Dear Parent:
Your child's love of reading starts here!

Every child learns to read in a different way and at his or her own speed. Some go back and forth between reading levels and read favorite books again and again. Others read through each level in order. You can help your young reader improve and become more confident by encouraging his or her own interests and abilities. From books your child reads with you to the first books he or she reads alone, there are I Can Read Books for every stage of reading:

SHARED READING
Basic language, word repetition, and whimsical illustrations, ideal for sharing with your emergent reader

BEGINNING READING
Short sentences, familiar words, and simple concepts for children eager to read on their own

READING WITH HELP
Engaging stories, longer sentences, and language play for developing readers

READING ALONE
Complex plots, challenging vocabulary, and high-interest topics for the independent reader

ADVANCED READING
Short paragraphs, chapters, and exciting themes for the perfect bridge to chapter books

I Can Read Books have introduced children to the joy of reading since 1957. Featuring award-winning authors and illustrators and a fabulous cast of beloved characters, I Can Read Books set the standard for beginning readers.

A lifetime of discovery begins with the magical words **"I Can Read!"**

Visit www.icanread.com for information
on enriching your child's reading experience.

I Can Read!™

READING 2 WITH HELP

IN A DARK, DARK ROOM
AND OTHER SCARY STORIES

RETOLD BY ALVIN SCHWARTZ
PICTURES BY VICTOR RIVAS

HARPER
An Imprint of HarperCollinsPublishers

To Calliope—A.S.

To Esther—V.R.

In a Dark, Dark Room and Other Scary Stories Text copyright © 1984 by Alvin Schwartz. Illustrations copyright © 2017 by Victor Rivas. All rights reserved. No part of this book may be used or reproduced in any manner whatsoever without written permission except in the case of brief quotations embodied in critical articles and reviews. Manufactured in U.S.A. For information address HarperCollins Children's Books, a division of HarperCollins Publishers, 195 Broadway, New York, NY 10007.
www.icanread.com

Library of Congress Control Number: 2016957933
ISBN 978-0-06-264338-4 (trade bdg.) — ISBN 978-0-06-264337-7 (pbk.)

Book design by Kathleen Duncan

17 18 19 20 LSCC 10 9 8 7 6 5 4 3
❖
Reillustrated edition, 2017

CONTENTS

FOREWORD

Most of us like scary stories

because we *like* feeling scared.

When there is no real danger,

feeling scared is fun.

The best times for these stories

is at night—

in front of a fire or in the dark.

Tell them s-l-o-w-l-y

and quietly,

and everyone will have

a good time.

9

THE TEETH

I was hurrying home in the dark

when I saw a man

walking toward me.

"Do you know what time it is?"

I asked.

The man lit a match

to look at his watch.

"It is eight o'clock," he said.

Then he grinned at me.

His teeth were three inches long!

When I saw them, I ran.

Soon I came to another man.

"Why are you running?"

the man asked.

"I just met a man

with teeth this long,"

I said.

"It scared me."

"My teeth are longer than that,"

said the man,

and he grinned at me.

When I saw his teeth, I ran.

Soon I came to another man.

"Why are you running?"

he asked me.

"I just saw a man

with teeth this long,"

I said.

"That's nothing," said the man.

"Did you ever see teeth *this* long?"

I took one look,

and I ran all the way home.

IN THE GRAVEYARD

A woman in a graveyard sat.

Ooooh!

Very short and very fat.

Ooooh!

She saw three corpses carried in.

Ooooh!

Very tall and very thin.

Ooooh!

To the corpses, the woman said,

"Will I be like you

when I am dead?"

Ooooh!

To the woman, the corpses said,
"You will be like us
when you are dead."
Ooooh!

To the corpses, the woman said,

"*AAAAAAAAAAAH!*"

THE GREEN RIBBON

Once there was a girl named Jenny.
She was like all the other girls,
except for one thing.
She always wore a green ribbon
around her neck.

There was a boy named Alfred
in her class.
Alfred liked Jenny,
and Jenny liked Alfred.

One day he asked her,

"Why do you wear that ribbon

all the time?"

"I cannot tell you," said Jenny.

But Alfred kept asking,

"Why *do* you wear it?"

And Jenny would say,

"It is not important."

Jenny and Alfred grew up
and fell in love.
One day they got married.

After their wedding,

Alfred said,

"Now that we are married,

you must tell me

about the green ribbon."

"You still must wait,"

said Jenny.

"I will tell you

when the right time comes."

Years passed.

Alfred and Jenny grew old.

One day Jenny became very sick.

The doctor told her

she was dying.

Jenny called Alfred to her side.

"Alfred," she said,

"now I can tell you

about the green ribbon.

Untie it,

and you will see

why I could not tell you before."

Slowly and carefully,

Alfred untied the ribbon,

and Jenny's head fell off.

IN A DARK, DARK ROOM

In a dark, dark wood,
there was a dark, dark house.

And in that dark, dark house,
there was a dark, dark room.

And in that dark, dark room,

there was a dark, dark chest.

And in that dark, dark chest,

there was a dark, dark shelf.

And on that dark, dark shelf,
there was a dark, dark box.
And in that dark, dark box,
there was—

THE NIGHT IT RAINED

It was late at night.

I was driving past the cemetery

when I saw a boy

standing in the rain.

"Do you want a ride home?"

I asked.

"Yes, please," he said.

"I live on Front Street,

next to the school."

I handed him my old sweater.

"It's cold tonight," I said.

"and you are wet.

You had better put this on."

After that, we did not talk.

When we stopped at his house,

I said,

"Keep the sweater.

I will get it tomorrow.

What is your name?"

"Jim," he said.

"Thanks for the ride."

I stopped for the sweater

the next day.

A woman came to the door.

"Is Jim at home?" I asked.

"I have come

to pick up my sweater."

She looked at me

in a strange way.

"It must have been another

boy,"

she said.

"Jim is our son.

But he has been dead

for almost a year.

He is buried in the cemetery."

I told her how sorry I was,

And I left.

I did not know what to think.

The next morning

I went to the cemetery.

I wanted to see Jim's grave.

Lying across the grave

was my sweater.

THE PIRATE

Ruth was spending her vacation
with her cousin Susan.

"A pirate once lived in our house,"
Susan told Ruth.
"He died in the room
where you are staying.
His ghost is supposed
to haunt that room.
But we have never seen it."
"I don't believe in ghosts,"
said Ruth.

But the thought of a pirate

haunting her room

scared her a little.

Before she got into bed that night,

Ruth looked everywhere.

She looked under the bed
and under the rug,

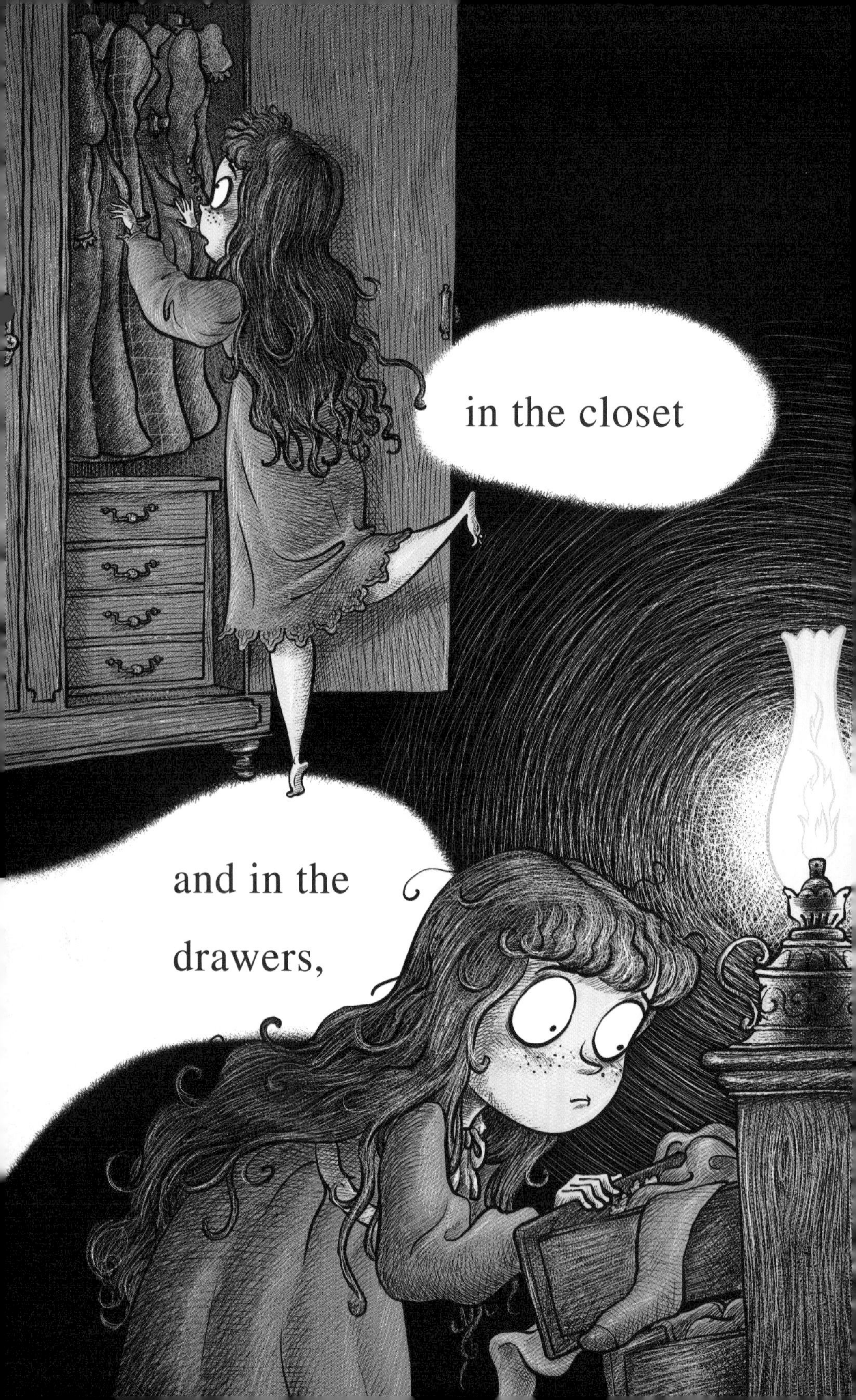
in the closet
and in the drawers,

behind the dresser

and behind the curtains,

and anywhere else a ghost might hide.

But she did not find a thing.

Ruth yawned and stretched

and got into bed.

She turned off the light

and snuggled under the covers.

"Just as I thought,"

she said to herself.

"There is no one in this room

but me."

Then a big voice said,

"And *ME!*"

THE GHOST OF JOHN

Have you seen the ghost of

John?

Long white bones

and the flesh all g-o-n-e?

Oooooooooh!

Wouldn't it be chilly

with no skin o-n?

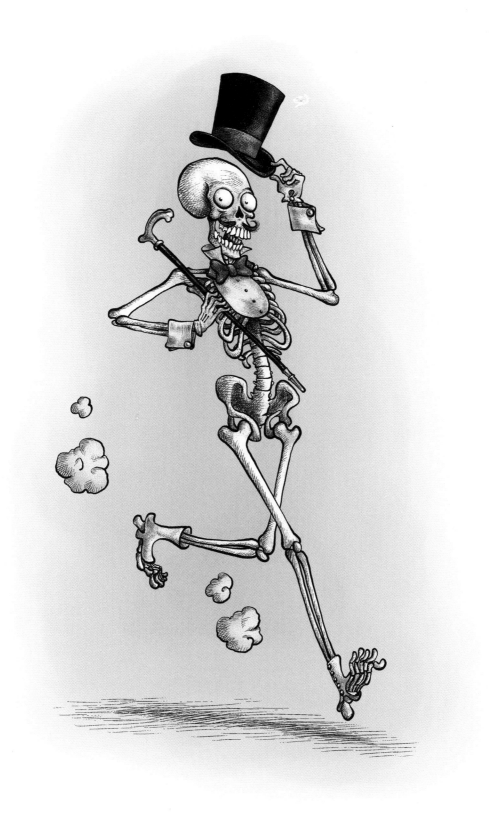

WHERE THE STORIES COME FROM

"The Teeth" is based on a story from Surinam (Dutch Guiana) collected in the 1920s by Melville and Frances Herskovitz.

"In the Graveyard" is a short version of the traditional song "Old Woman All Skin and Bone."

"The Green Ribbon" is based on a European folk motif in which a red thread is worn around a person's neck. The thread marks the place where the head was cut off, then reattached.

"In a Dark, Dark Room" is known in England and America.

"The Night It Rained" is based on variants of the widespread folktale "The Ghostly Hitchhiker."

"The Pirate" is based on a reference in *A Dictionary of British Folk-Tales in the English Language* by Katharine M. Briggs, v. 3, p. 416.

"The Ghost of John" was collected by the compiler in 1979 from Lynette M. Lee, age 8, Stockton, California.

ABOUT THE AUTHOR

Alvin Schwartz compiled over two dozen books of folklore for young readers that explored everything from wordplay and humor tales to legends of all kinds. His I Can Read books included *I Saw You in the Bathroom and Other Folk Rhymes* and *Ghosts: Ghostly Tales from Folklore*. He's also written three very popular collections of scary stories—*Scary Stories to Tell in the Dark*, *More Scary Stories to Tell in the Dark*, and *Scary Stories 3*.

ABOUT THE ILLUSTRATOR

Victor Rivas was born and raised in Vigo, Spain, and now lives outside of Barcelona. He has been a freelance illustrator since 1987, illustrating books for children and teens. Victor enjoys creating comics, animation, films, and games, as well as spending time with his daughter, Marta.